A Day in the Life of Tommy

Based on the TV series Rugrats® created by Arlene Klasky,
Gabor Csupo Inc. and Paul Germain as seen on BBC tv

First published in Great Britain in 1999 by Simon & Schuster UK Ltd
Africa House, 64-78 Kingsway, London WC2B 6AH
Copyright © 1999 Viacom International Inc.
All rights reserved. NICKELODEON, Rugrats, and all related titles,
logos, and characters are trademarks of Viacom International Inc.

A CIP catalogue for this book is available from the British Library
ISBN 0-671-02872-3
Manufactured in the United States of America

1 3 5 7 9 10 8 6 4 2

A Day in the Life of Tommy

by David Lewman

POCKET
BOOKS

Table of Contents

Hi! I'm Tommy Pickles. You can call me
Tommy. I have lots of adventures every day.
C'mon, I'll show you!

Wake Up!

The first thing I do every morning is wake up.
How do I wake up? Well, um, I just stop
sleeping. Then I wake up! Sometimes I
play in my cot for a little while. There's
lots of fun things to do, like

- Talk to Reptar
- Try to reach my mobile
- Get under my blanket and see how dark it gets
- Grab the bars and pretend I'm an aminal in a zoo

And how do I know when it's time
to get up and start having adventures?
When the sun starts to climb up out of its
bed, it's time!

Here's how to get a growed-up to lift you
out of your cot:
- Talk into the little white box with the red light
- Rattle the bars of your cot (I use my rattle.)
- Cry really loud!
  But if they're too sleepy to hear you,
  just let yourself out—with a screwdriver
  or your blanket!

What to Wear

After you get out of your cot, the first thing
you gotta do is get dressed. You can't stay in
your pajamas all day because . . . um, uh . . .
I don't know why, but you can't. The growed-
ups won't let you. And you can't be nakie all
day either—unless you're Spike. And even
he wears a collar!

Here's what I wear:
- A clean diapie. If you're not sure whether the diapie is clean, just smell it. Then you'll know for sure! Oh, it's important to wear diapies that fit. Otherwise your diapie will fall down, and then it gets a little chilly.
- A blue T-shirt. Mine is loose and comfy.
- No shoes—so I can always feel mud squelch between my toes! Now I'm ready to go!

Everybody Tommy-cise!

To do what a baby's gotta do, a baby's gotta get in shape. Here we go!

The first part of our big workout is crawling. Let's crawl . . .
- under the kitchen table
- behind the couch
- and around the playpen three times

Now let's do a few laps. First Mummy's lap . . . then Daddy's lap . . . then Grandpa Lou's lap! The more laps, the better!

The next part of our workout is grabbing and pulling. First you grab, then you pull yourself up. Let's grab . . .
- the TV
- Spike
- and the tablecloth

Good job! Now that we're warmed up, we can play with my toys!

My Toys

Welcome to this tour of my toys! Please keep your hands inside my room at all times.

On your right, or maybe your left, you'll see a fun toy—a jack-in-the-box! But Chuckie thinks it's scary.

Behind the jack-in-the-box are a lot of blocks. These are for stacking up so you can knock 'em down. They've got pictures on 'em, but nobody knows what the pictures mean.

Here is my toy boat. Can you say toy boat three times really fast? Neither can I. I like to have this boat with me when I have a bath. In this boat, we can sail the bubbly seas!

And last on our tour is my favouritest toy in the world, my ball. It's the star of my collection. Okay, the tour's over, 'cause that's the way the ball bounces!

Dil's Skills

Now that I got a little brother, I gotta be a good BIG brother and teach Dil all the things I knowed! One of the most importantest things growed-ups like babies to learn is to make aminal sounds. So I'm gonna teach Dil to make sounds.

"Okay, Dil. What does the cow say?"

"Goo!"

"That's close! The cow says, 'Moo'! Can you say 'Moo'?"

"Gaa gaa!"

"No . . . 'Mooooo'!"

"Baa boo!"

"Dil, the cow says—ouch! Please don't hit me with that!"

"Yow yow yow yow."

"Um, maybe you can say 'baaaa' like a sheep."
"Goo."
"Tweet-tweet?"
"Gaa."
"Meow?"
"Blah bloh. Bloo."
"Hmm . . . okay, Dilly. What does a BABY say?"
"Goo goo ga ga!"
"Yay, Dil!"

A Baby's Best Friend

Now that Dil's had his lesson
(I think he's really smart,
don't you?), it's time to
take care of our fambly
dog, Spike! There are a
lot of important things
I have to do for
Spike, like

- Taste his food to make sure it's okay
- Exercise him by riding on his back
- Make sure he doesn't sleep too much
- Dry his tongue off with my face
- Play tug-of-war with him (we use his lead)
- Check to see if any of his spots are missing
- Help him practice his howls
- If he's tired of walking, get behind and push
- If he feels like running, get behind and hang on!

The Never-Stinky Diapie and Other Great Inventions

Now let's go down to the basement and see what my dad is making today! He makes all kinds of great toys. Some of them work. Here are other things I think he should make too:

• The Reptar Whistle. Blow this whistle, and Reptar would come visit!

• The De-Broccoli-izer. Point this at your bowl and *zap*! No more broccoli!

• The Worm Locater. Walk around the garden with this, and it would beep every time you got near a worm! Phil and Lil would like that.

• The Clown Alarm. This one's for Chuckie 'cause he's afraid of clowns. The alarm would go off whenever a clown is near.

•The Never-Stinky Diapie. You'd never have to change it!

•The Seeyoulater. When your friends have to go home, just turn on the Seeyoulater, and they'd come right back!

•The Bottomless Bottle. No matter how long you drink, this bottle would never be empty!

•The Angelica Nice-ifier. Stick this on Angelica's head, flip the switch, and she'd turn nice!

•The Adventuretron 2000. Push the button, and your day would be full of adventures! (But I don't really need this!)

Angelica

My cousin
Angelica is three
years old. She's a bit
mean sometimes. But
even though we don't have
an Angelica Nice-ifier
right now, here's what to
do when she comes over.

- Push all the toys under the
  cot so she won't take 'em.
- Tell her how prettyful she looks. She likes that.
- Ask Susie Carmichael for help. She always
  knows what to do.
- Point to somewhere behind her and say,
  "Look, Angelica! A bucket full of biscuits!"
  Then when she looks, run away really fast.
  When do you say it?
  NOW!

A Closer Look

Whew! That was close, but we got away from Angelica. Now what should we do? Hey, let's play with my magdifrying glass! Can you tell what I'm looking at?

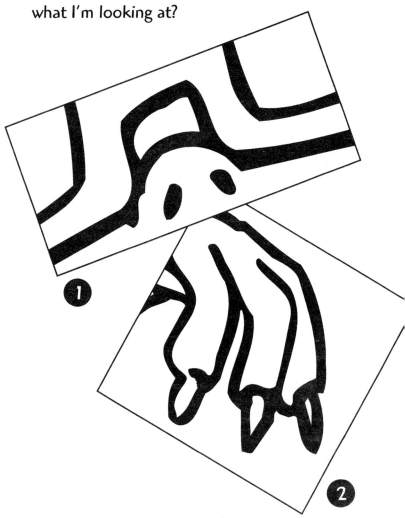

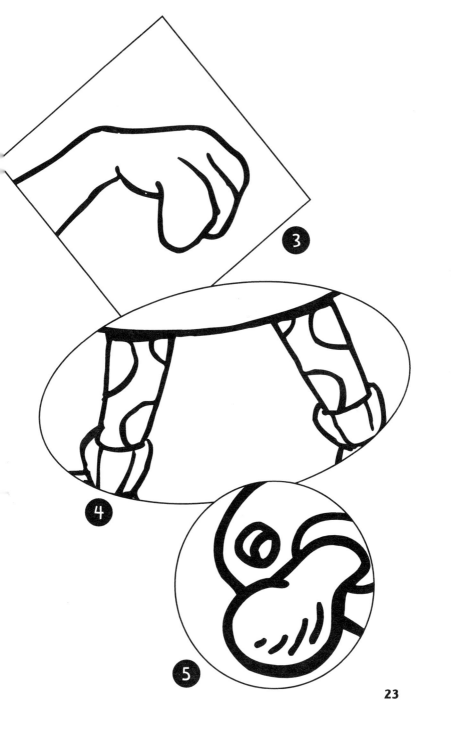

3

4

5

23

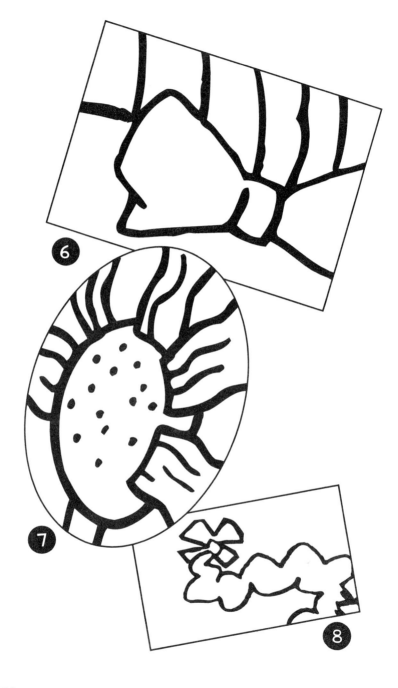

6

7

8

24

1. Chuckie's nose and the bottom of his glasses
2. Reptar's claw
3. Spike's paw
4. Angelica's polka-dot tights
5. Dil's pacifier
6. Lil's hair bow and hair
7. The back of Cynthia's head
8. Susie's pigtail
9. Didi's earring
10. Stu's stubble

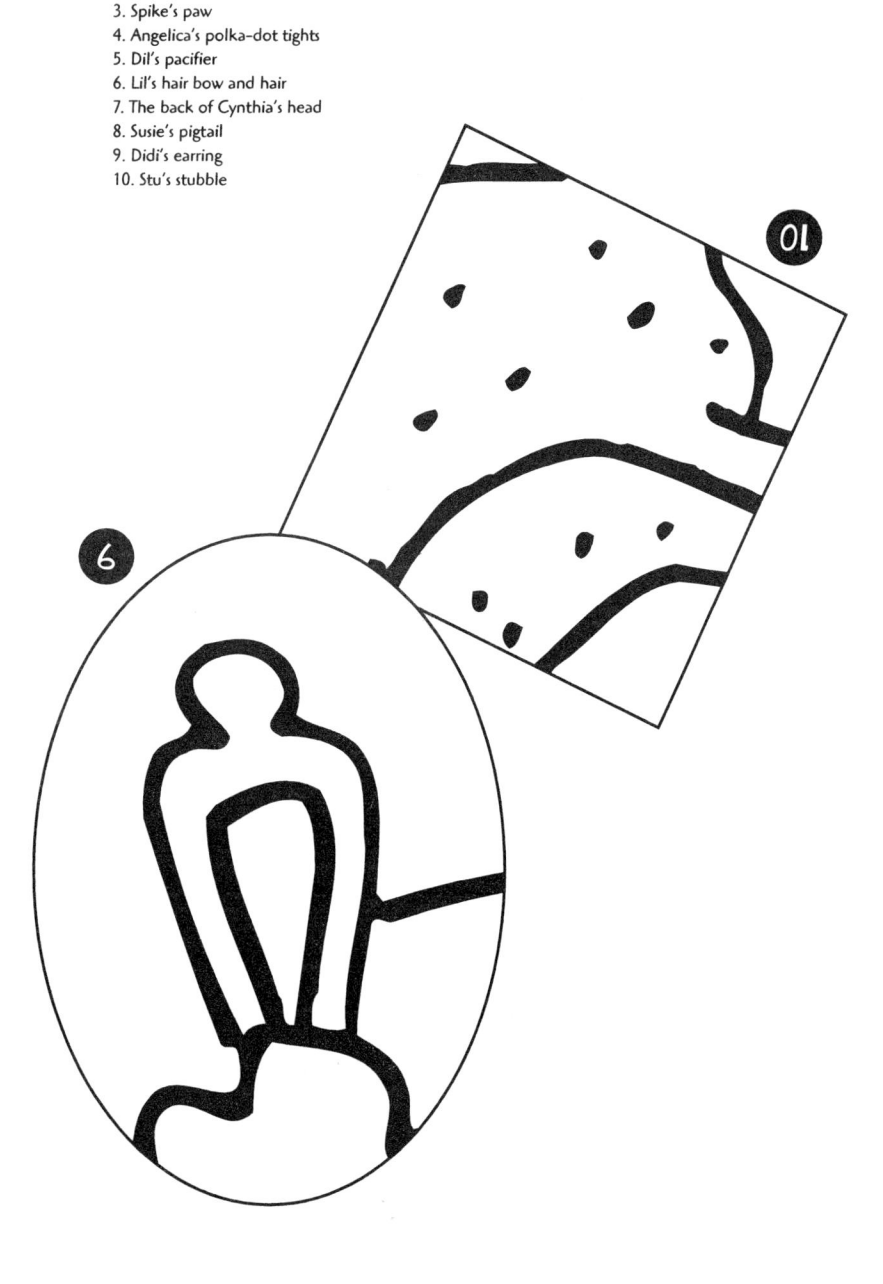

Reptar Rules!

Reptar is my favouritest monster. And when I meet him, I will

- Climb up his back to reach the biscuits
- Ride him to the park
- Play hide-and-seek

- Ask him about his TV show
- See if he can get tickets to "Reptar on Ice"
- Ask him to help pick up big heavy rocks so
  Phil and Lil can look for worms underneath them
- Make him scare Angelica (just a little!)

Growed-Ups

Growed-ups are different from babies. They're bigger, and they do funny things sometimes. So every baby's gotta know the dos and don'ts of being around them, like

DO play with toys as soon as they give 'em to you. DON'T play with the channel thing while they're watching TV.

DO stay in the playpen until they leave the room. DON'T forget to keep a screwdriver handy so you can escape.

DO crawl on their laps for a hug.
DON'T pull on the newspaper while trying to reach their laps.

DO try out your dad's new invention.
DON'T be the first one to try it out.

DO jump into their arms if they stretch them towards you.
DON'T jump into their arms when they're cooking dinner.

DO wiggle if they turn on some music.
DON'T wiggle while they're pinning your diaper.

DO play "horsie" on their knees.
DON'T play "horsie" on their heads.

DO point to things you want them to give you.
DON'T point to your cot if you're not sleepy.

DO rub your head on their tummies.
DON'T rub your food in their hair.

DO wipe your feet on their doormats.
DON'T wipe your nose on their shirts.

DO show them what you drawed on paper.
DON'T show them what you drawed on the walls.

DO bring them pretty flowers from the garden.
DON'T bring them pretty bugs from the garden.

DO let them leave you with your grandpa.
DON'T let them leave you with your cousin!

Life's an Adventure!

When you're a baby, there's always something to do, like

• Go for a ride

• Make music

- Pretend I'm in a munching band

- Blow bubbles

- Trade places

33

•Fix something

•Play with your brother

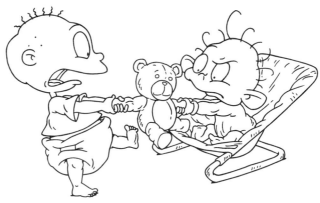

•Dance

• Study aminals

• Even try an asperiment!

Phil and Lil Make Lunch

Are you hungry? I am! Let's have Phil and Lil make us something to eat. Pick what you want from this menu; Phil and Lil will pick it from where they find it!

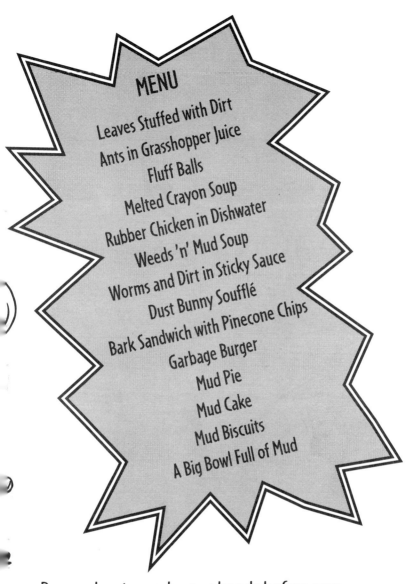

MENU

Leaves Stuffed with Dirt

Ants in Grasshopper Juice

Fluff Balls

Melted Crayon Soup

Rubber Chicken in Dishwater

Weeds 'n' Mud Soup

Worms and Dirt in Sticky Sauce

Dust Bunny Soufflé

Bark Sandwich with Pinecone Chips

Garbage Burger

Mud Pie

Mud Cake

Mud Biscuits

A Big Bowl Full of Mud

Remember to wash your hands before you
eat—and after, too!

Tommy Pickles, Sports Hero

Someday I want to be a sports hero! But first you gots to learn the rules.

• In football you can throw, kick, or carry the ball, but you can't bite it . . .

unless you're Reptar.

•In hockey the goalie should always wear a
mask. Even if it isn't Halloween.

• In baseball, if a dog runs away with the ball, that's called a "bone run."

• Whoever gets to the ball first, kicks it. Whoever gets there last . . . doesn't!

The Bestest Art I Ever Drawed

After playing in the park, I like to play inside.
What should we do? I know, let's make some art.

If you don't know what to draw, draw your bestest
friend!

Or if you've got some clay, you can make a
stachoo of your friend!

When you paint, you don't have to use a
brush. You can use your hands!

And when you want to draw a big picture of a friend, you can use chalk to draw on the driveway. Of course, if your friend is Reptar, you'll need a really big driveway!

A Tommy Story

Before I fall asleep, I like to hear a
bedtime story. Here's a story my dad
told me. At least, this is the way I
remember it:

Once upon a time there was a brave knight
named Sir Tommy. He was riding his mighty

stallion Spike through the
woods when a scary old
witch stopped him.
"Marry me," said the
scary old witch, "or I'll
turn you into a frog."
"I can't get married," said Sir Tommy, "I'm
just a baby." So the witch turned him into a
frog and left him in a pond.

Pretty soon a royal
party came from
the castle to have
a picnic by the pond.
"Look!" said Lady Lil,
"A baby frog!"
"Let's play with it,"
said Sir Phil. "Maybe we'll get warts."

But the royal wizard,
Chucklin the Careful, said,
"That's no frog. That's my
bestest friend, Sir Tommy!
See the seven hairs on his head?
He must be under a spill!"
Sir Phil said, "To break a frog
spill, he's gotta be kissed by the princess!"
The proud Princess Angelica said, "Kiss a yucky
frog? No way!"
"You gotta kiss him," said Lady Lil. "He's the
only one that can save Prince Dil from Reptar
the Dragon."
"Reptar, eh?" said the princess. "All right, but

he's gotta bring me
the dragon's treasure—
Reptar bars!" She gave
the frog a quick kiss—
"Yuck!"—and the frog
turned back into Sir
Tommy.
"Thank you, Princess
Angelica," said Sir
Tommy. "Now I gotta
save Prince Dil!"

Then he jumped on his mighty stallion Spike and rode off to Reptar's cave. "Reptar the Dragon," called Sir Tommy, "you gotta give Prince Dil back right now!"

"Sure," said Reptar, "we were just playing. You want some Reptar bars?"

"Yeah!" said Sir Tommy.

So Sir Tommy took Prince Dil and a whole lot of Reptar bars back to the castle. Everybody ate the Reptar bars. Princess Angelica ate so many that she got a very bad tummyache and had to spend many days in bed. The end.

Wow! That was my bestest day ever! And you know what? Tomorrow will be even better. See you in the morning—bright and early.

Good-bye!